Trixie
The Witch's Cat

Nick Butterworth

PUFFIN

Trixie, the witch's cat, was a happy cat. Most of the time. There was only one thing that could make Trixie really unhappy and, luckily, it was something Trixie didn't think about.

Most of the time.

But then, sometimes, Trixie just couldn't help it.

Then, Trixie the happy cat, became Trixie the very-unhappy-indeed cat.

She would go into a bad mood, as if a dark thundercloud had settled over her head.

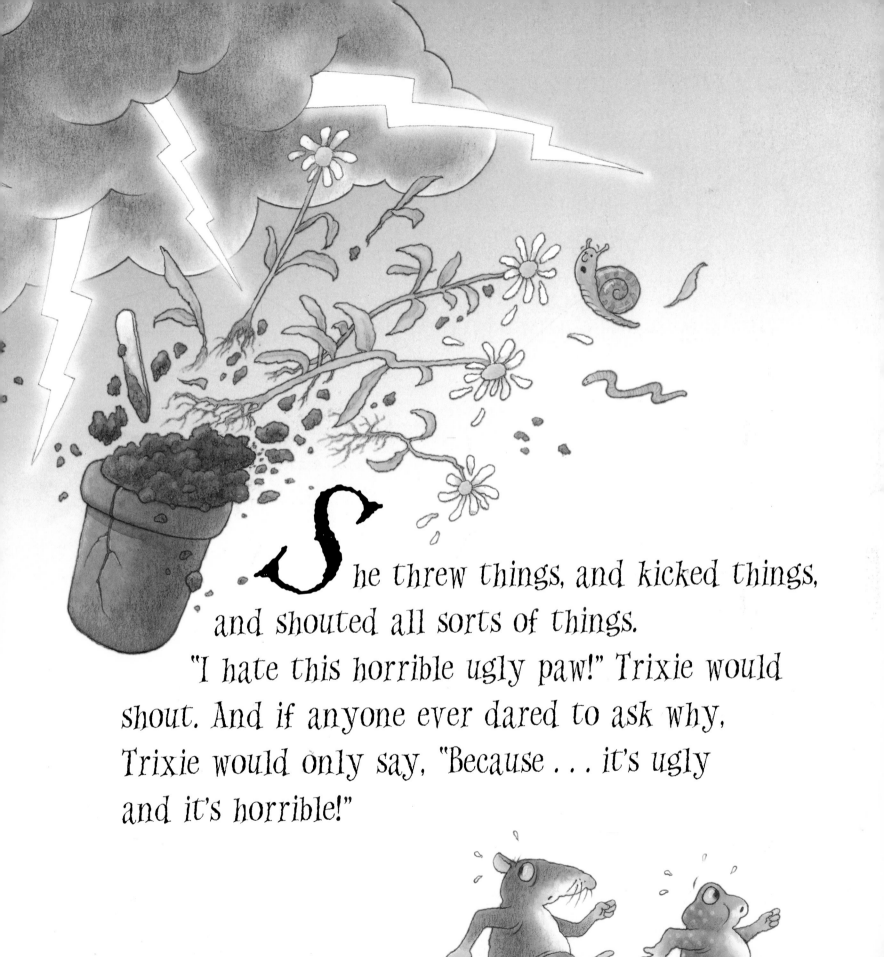

She threw things, and kicked things, and shouted all sorts of things.

"I hate this horrible ugly paw!" Trixie would shout. And if anyone ever dared to ask why, Trixie would only say, "Because . . . it's ugly and it's horrible!"

Trixie's "horrible, ugly paw" was really a very nice paw. It was the right size and shape and the claws worked properly. It was beautifully fluffy and it was . . . white.

And that was the problem. Trixie knew for certain that witches' cats did not have white paws, because . . . because . . . Well, they just didn't.

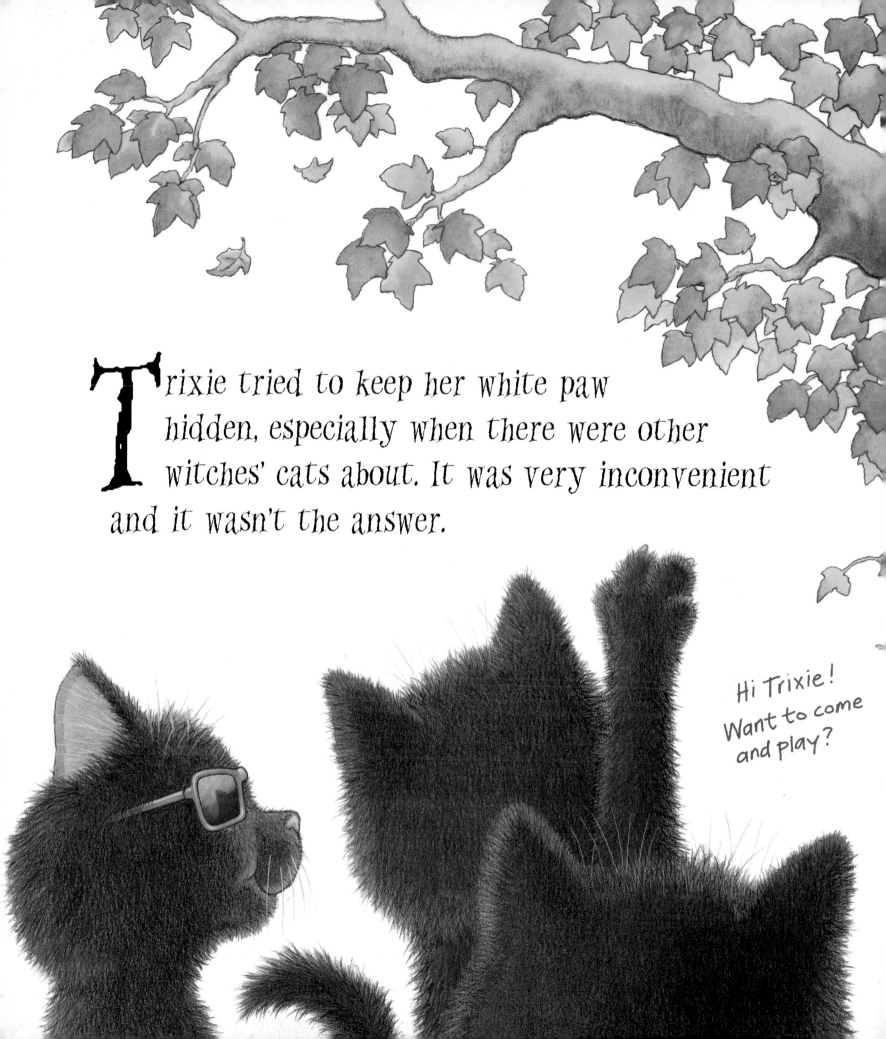

Trixie tried to keep her white paw hidden, especially when there were other witches' cats about. It was very inconvenient and it wasn't the answer.

Hi Trixie! Want to come and play?

At last, after one really bad-mood-thundercloud-throwing-things-and-kicking-things-and-shouting-things kind of day, Trixie decided that something just had to be done about THAT PAW. She had a plan.

"I'm going to completely stop washing this paw," she said. "Then it will get dirtier and dirtier and dirtier."

Trixie thought if she left it long enough,
it would go nice and black, like her other paws.
"I'm not going to wash it for a hundred years,"
she said.

At first, Trixie was pleased with her plan. She stopped washing her paw and it did get dirtier and dirtier.

But it didn't go black. And after only three weeks of her one hundred years, Trixie's paw began to smell. Badly. REALLY badly.

Trixie had an idea that she
would paint her paw black.
It was NOT a good idea.

Suddenly, Trixie had another idea. A brilliant idea, she thought. "Of course!" she said. "I'm a witch's cat. I'll use MAGIC to turn my paw black!"

First, Trixie borrowed the witch's wand and her book of spells. Then she got busy with a very important piece of magic . . .

ONE PINCH OF BLACK PEPPER.
   BLACK HAIR FROM CAT'S FOOT.
TWO BLACKBIRD FEATHERS.
   THREE BUCKETS OF SOOT.
BLACK TREACLE.
   BLACKBERRIES,
      THIRTEEN TIMES TWO.
BUBBLE AND BOIL IN A
      BLACK
         WITCHY
            BREW.

Suddenly . . .

rixie was amazed to find that she had not
been hurt. She could easily comb her hair over
a little bald patch on top of her head where
she had lost some fur. But as she looked into
the mirror, Trixie was even
more amazed.

She was delighted to see that her white paw was black! Her magic had worked! Hooray! At last, Trixie was a proper black witch's cat. Just like all the others.

But, oh dear. Now it was impossible to tell which one of the witch's cats was Trixie and which one wasn't.

No one could say which witch's cat was which.
Without her white paw, even Trixie wondered
which one she was.

It was then that Trixie began
to miss her old white paw.
Her nice white paw.
Her lovely white paw.
She really did. And now
it was gone. Forever.

Trixie started
to cry.

As Trixie wiped away a tear with her new black paw, something very strange happened. The black began to fade. First, to dark grey . . .

. . . snowy white! What was going on?
Was it just that Trixie's magic was not very
strong? Or could it be there was some
stronger magic in Trixie's tears?

...then to light grey,
then lighter and lighter,
until Trixie's paw was...

rixie had no idea.
   She only knew that her white paw,
      which was just the right size and shape,
her paw with its properly working claws,
her perfectly beautiful, fluffy, WHITE paw,
was back where it belonged.

From that day, Trixie never again went into
a bad mood, or threw things, or kicked things,
         or shouted things. Well ... hardly ever.
               And never EVER about ...
                  that paw.

Trixie was happy to be
just the way she was.

For someone very special . . .

Will you be like Mummy? Daddy? Harry? Grandad Joe?
Grandma? Grandad? Granny? Mooch? It's hard for us to know?
One, or some, or none of these? We haven't got a clue,
But one thing is quite certain . . . you're going to be like you.

. . . with heaps of love from Grandpa

PUFFIN BOOKS
Published by the Penguin Group: London, New York, Australia,
Canada, India, Ireland, New Zealand and South Africa
Penguin Books Ltd, Registered Offices:
80 Strand, London WC2R 0RL, England

puffinbooks.com

First published 2009
1 3 5 7 9 10 8 6 4 2
Copyright © Nick Butterworth, 2009
Printed in China
ISBN: 978-0-141-32680-1